Dear Pat —

Thank you for all the kindnesses you've shown to me & my children

May God Bless You!

Love

Passing Thoughts…
To Ponder

&

A Tribute to
Women and Romance

by

David M. Rosso, M.D.

authorHOUSE™

1663 LIBERTY DRIVE, SUITE 200
BLOOMINGTON, INDIANA 47403
(800) 839-8640
WWW.AUTHORHOUSE.COM

First published by AuthorHouse 12/08/04

ISBN: 1-4184-9396-1 (e)
ISBN: 1-4184-9395-3 (sc)
ISBN: 1-4184-9394-5 (dj)

Printed in the United States of America
Bloomington, Indiana

This book is printed on acid-free paper.

Passing Thoughts...
...To Ponder...

Passing Thoughts...
To Ponder

&

A Tribute to

Women

and

Romance

This book is dedicated
To my children...
Kristen and Michael...
May you both maintain your spirit of youth
While developing the wisdom
That comes with age...
May God grant you strength in adversity...
Hope in despair...
Solace in sorrow...
And peace in the knowledge
That sunsets...
Are always followed
By sunrises...

I Love You!
God Bless You!

...Daddy

Passing Thoughts…
To Ponder

&

A Tribute to

Women

and

Romance

Fall is a beautiful time of year…
Leaves…once vibrant green,
Basking in the summer sun,
Now…as they begin their well-deserved slumber…
Their work completed…
Their gifts…providing nourishment to their immediate world
And joy to all that surrounds it…given…
Begin to reveal their inner beauty…
Radiant reds and shimmering golds begin to dot the landscape…
And as the great circle of life continues
In all its splendor and wonder…
The canvas becomes enveloped in these awe-inspiring pigments
They cast a magical spell…briefly…
And then peacefully…with quiet dignity…return to the earth
To provide their very essence to the promises of spring

Passing Thoughts... To Ponder

&

A Tribute to Women and Romance

We are far better off if we allow our hearts to make the decision
…After appropriate counsel from our minds,
Rather than allowing our minds to make the decision

Intelligence resides in the mind…
Wisdom resides in the heart

Knowledge helps us to make the right decision…
Humility, oftentimes, prevents us from making the wrong decision

Passing Thoughts…
To Ponder

&

A Tribute to
Women
and
Romance

The dawn of a new day
Brings renewed hope
That the sun may set over a better world…
A kinder, more peaceful world…
Beginning with our own small corner of it…
It all begins one person at a time…

In nature…
There are laws…
And every living thing…
Except people…
Follow them

Think of how much happier
We would all be…
If we would
Simply follow
The laws of nature

Passing Thoughts… To Ponder

&

A Tribute to

Women

and

Romance

I've been practicing medicine for about ten years…
And every time I see a healthy newborn baby,
My mind marvels at the miracle
I hold in my hands

One would think that such an event
Would become "routine" after such a period of time…
But, let me assure you…there is nothing routine
About the greatest miracle of all…

My father, the greatest man I've known, once said,
"Work is doing something you don't enjoy"…
…I am blessed in that I haven't 'worked' in the past ten years

We have a great many things to teach our children…
We have a great many things to learn from our children…

Passing Thoughts…
To Ponder

&

A Tribute to

Women

and

Romance

I believe that the book, _The Little Prince_,
Should be required reading for every freshman college student…

Let us not be consumed with "matters of consequence"…
Let us, rather, maintain our ability to view life
Through the eyes of a child

Adults tend to look 'through' everything toward a perceived goal…
To a child…the only goal is the 'everything' in the way…

…Do not be so intent on the goal, that the 'everything' becomes
overlooked

Passing Thoughts...
To Ponder

&

A Tribute to

Women

and

Romance

Some of life's most cherished moments
Resound with the echoes of silence

Let us take lessons from nature…
Times of growth are always followed by
Times of rest

Strength stems from failure…
Success stems from strength

Passing Thoughts...
To Ponder

&

A Tribute to

Women

and

Romance

Why do so many people...
Try to outrun their guardian angels?

Think of all the good
That could be accomplished...
If the time spent complaining
About the problems that exist...
Were spent on trying to solve them...

The merit of a good deed
Lies not in its magnitude...
But rather...
In the sacrifice involved...

Passing Thoughts...
To Ponder

&

A Tribute to

Women

and

Romance

Beauty in this world is plentiful…
Those who take the time to appreciate it…blessed

The smiling face of a child…
Outshines even the most brilliant of sunrises

The silence created
In a child's absence…
Is deafening

Passing Thoughts…
To Ponder

&

A Tribute to

Women

and

Romance

It's remarkable that a child's expression
Corresponds so closely to their actual feelings…

Somewhere along the line,
We begin our preparation of various masks
Which are painstakingly cared for,
And frequently, far too easily retrievable

These masks, at times,
Are appropriate…for short periods…
However, the wearer occasionally
Becomes so adept at their application…
They become preferred to communication

Effective communication
Eliminates the excessive utilization of these masks…
And may dismantle several of them entirely…

…Let us regain the spirit of the child within us
While maintaining the wisdom that comes with age

Passing Thoughts…
To Ponder

&

A Tribute to

Women

and

Romance

What is the secret
To maintain the wonder of youth?

All too often,
We become deadened to the beauty which surrounds us…
We have lost our focus…
We have become consumed by things of fleeting value…
Rather than placing primary importance
On moments
Which have the potential to warm the heart
Through eternity…

We once knew…
As children…
How to take advantage of those moments…
Instinctively…

Yet, as adults…
This gift must be either nurtured…or lost…
Once lost…it is very difficult,
Yet not impossible,
To regain…

Passing Thoughts...
To Ponder

&

A Tribute to

Women

and

Romance

We are interesting creatures…

As the day passes,
We may feel, at times, that we are in control
Of our own destiny…
At other times,
We may feel anxious when we feel our sense of control
Start to waiver…

There are those who spend their entire life…
Fluctuating…
Between one extreme and the other…

If the truth be known…
No justification exists
For either extreme…

This evening…regard the sunset…
In its quiet majesty,
This will become apparent…
And anxiety will be replaced…
With peace…

Passing Thoughts…
To Ponder

&

A Tribute to

Women

and

Romance

Le coucher de soleil…
Ca…c'est vrai…
Le jour…c'est perdu,
Mais pas oublie'…

Et demain…quand le soleil reviendra…
Aujourd'hui
Ne sera qu'une memoire…
Dans l'esprit…
Et dans l'ame…

Car le soleil ne se couche
Que dans l'ame…
Et ne se leve
Que dans l'espoire…

Passing Thoughts...
To Ponder

&

A Tribute to
Women
and
Romance

(Translation)

The sun is setting…
And although it is true
That the day is over…
It is not forgotten…

And tomorrow,
When the sun returns…
Today will be but a memory
In the spirit…
And in the soul…

For the sun does not set
But in the soul…
And does not rise
But in hope…

Passing Thoughts…
To Ponder

&

A Tribute to

Women

and

Romance

Si on regarde le coucher de soleil
Avec les yeux…
On ne voie que les couleurs…

Mais…si on le regarde avec le coeur…
On voie beaucoup plus…

La radiance de l'amour de Dieu
Qui cascade du ciel
Et qui remplie le ciel
Pour nous rappeler
De la beaute'
De la vie…

Passing Thoughts…
To Ponder

&

A Tribute to

Women

and

Romance

(Translation)

If one watches the setting sun
With the eyes...
One doesn't see but colors...

However, if one watches with the heart...
One sees much more...

The radiance of God's love
Which cascades from Heaven
And which fills the sky
To remind us
Of the beauty
Of life...

Passing Thoughts…
To Ponder

&

A Tribute to
Women
and
Romance

All too often, women associate beauty
With virtually impossible physical standards…

Among the most attractive women whom I've known in my life
Are those whose spirit and quiet confidence shone from their eyes
In irresistible fashion…
It is a compelling attraction
That transcends physical nature
…They exude the very essence of all that it is to be a woman

Simply because society has finally accepted the obvious fact
That women are equally competent as men;
That does not imply that they should be treated
As anything less than a woman…
Let us celebrate the inherent differences…
Let us remember that chivalry
Is a sign of respect…

Passing Thoughts...
To Ponder

&

A Tribute to
Women
and
Romance

My Lady...
I was thinking of you this evening...
And I don't even know your name
The exact color of your eyes escapes me...
As does the tint of your hair...
But, I can see your heart...
Vividly...
And I know your soul

We haven't even met...yet...
But we will...
I know not the day...
Nor the hour...
Nor the place...
But...when our eyes meet...
We will recognize each other...
And our hearts shall breathe
A peaceful sigh...
As when one, at last, finds something
For which they've long searched...

...And we shall be home...

Passing Thoughts...
To Ponder

&

A Tribute to
Women
and
Romance

My Dear Lady…
I saw the setting sun this evening…
And I thought of you…

Its brilliant rays shining through a narrow break in the clouds…
Turned orange and pink from its splendor

I've seen a narrow band of rays
Emanating from your heart…
Surrounded by the clouds of fear and hesitation
Which have developed over time's passage
…The radiance is exquisite…
And a brief prelude of the full magnificence which exists…
And which shall be revealed…
…As the fear dissipates…
With the warmth of summer's day

Passing Thoughts…
To Ponder

&

A Tribute to
Women
and
Romance

The rose unfolds its petals…
Slowly…
Patiently…

If one attempts…
In their zeal
To smell its sweet fragrance…
To open the petals before their time…
The rose will wither…
The petals will fall…
And its fragrance…lost…

Roses require patience…
How does one balance
Patience with passion?

The answer
Is now clear…
"Passionate patience"…

Yet, have the petals
Begun to fall?

Passing Thoughts...
To Ponder

&

A Tribute to

Women

and

Romance

Children's Corner

During my career as a pediatrician, I've been blessed
With the opportunity to spend my days
With the most delightful people on earth…
Children

Here is just a sampling of the sometimes humorous,
Oftentimes insightful remarks
Which have added smiles
To my life…

Passing Thoughts...
To Ponder

&

A Tribute to
Women
and
Romance

Question: "You're five years old? When will you turn six?
Response: "On my birthday."

   ... Children often see the obvious when adults fail to do so

Question: "Who's your best friend?"
Response: "My mommy."

Question: "What's your favorite part of first grade?"
Response: "Going home!"

Passing Thoughts…
To Ponder

&

A Tribute to
Women
and
Romance

Question: "Does your throat hurt?"

Response: "If I say yes, are you going to put that stick down my throat?"

Question: "Do you like your new baby sister?"

Response: "She's okay, I guess. I asked Santa for a brother, but they must have been all out of boys."

Question: "Do you like your teacher?"

Response: "No. She's mean!"

Question: "What does she do that's mean?"

Response: "She makes us pay attention, and she gives us homework!"

...A proper perspective always requires a degree of distance

Passing Thoughts…
To Ponder

&

A Tribute to

Women

and

Romance

Question: "What do you want to be when you grow up?"
Response: "A doctor, and a teacher, and a hockey player."

...A child's dream has no knowledge of the 24-hour day

Question: "What do you want to be when you grow up?"
Response: "A mommy...just like my mommy!"

...There exists no greater testimonial

Question: "What do you want to be when you grow up?"
Response: "I don't want to grow up! I want to stay a kid!"

...Fortunately, the heart has the ability to remain young

Passing Thoughts…
To Ponder

&

A Tribute to
Women
and
Romance

I was examining a baby, and his precious 6 year old sister was seated quietly on the other side of the room. I turned to her, and asked, "What do you want to be when you grow up?" She sighed softly and replied, "I haven't decided yet. I've got too much on my plate right now."

After chuckling with her parents for a minute, I turned to her and said, "But, honey, you're only 6 years old. You're too young to even have a plate!"

... Children will never cease to amaze you!

Passing Thoughts…
To Ponder

&

A Tribute to
Women
and
Romance

Parents' Corner

This section is dedicated to the profession of parenthood...
The most difficult and the most rewarding profession in the world...

To all those who raise children...you are blessed...

May God continue to bless you
With peace and love,
Courage and compassion,
Strength and gentleness...
And many priceless memories...

Passing Thoughts...
To Ponder

&

A Tribute to
Women
and
Romance

When my daughter was four years old and my son was seven…
I read to them a children's book which discussed, in basic terms,
The four essential requirements for a plant to flourish
(Soil, water, sunlight, and gases from the air)

Several weeks later, I was showing my daughter a house plant
Which was blossoming…
I asked her if she remembered the things which a plant required
In order to grow…

She hesitated and pondered…
Then slowly answered…
"Dirt…water…the sun…"
I replied, "Very good! There's one more thing…
Can you remember it?"…

She paused for a few seconds…
Then…a proud smile illuminated her face,
And she confidently replied…
"Love!"

"…From the mouths of babes…"

Passing Thoughts...
To Ponder

&

A Tribute to
Women
and
Romance

I once asked my seven year old son
If he would prefer to stay with me for Sunday dinner
Or to go have dinner with his friend…

He started to answer…then hesitated…
Looked at me…and replied…
"Would you feel lonely if I went to my friend's?"

…What did I ever do to deserve such a son?…

…Children are far more insightful than for which they are credited

Passing Thoughts...
To Ponder

&

A Tribute to

Women

and

Romance

Last week, I held my four year old daughter in my arms
With her head on my shoulder
And danced with her…

I know that there will be a day
When I will be dancing with her again…
…though in my arms
I will be holding a woman

I'm certain…at that moment…
I will close my eyes
And re-live
One very special dance
When I held a little angel in my arms…

My heart will fill with a joyous ache
And tears of time-nourished love
Will cloud my sight
As I regard a vision of Heaven…
While remembering
A blessed moment on earth

Passing Thoughts...
To Ponder

&

A Tribute to
Women
and
Romance

I was watching my son at soccer practice one day,
And his little sister, who was almost 5 at the time,
Was in front of me
Picking dandelions tirelessly…

At one point, I looked down…
And she had a huge bouquet
Clutched in her little hand…

As she continued
About her loving task…
She asked me…
"Daddy, how many dandelions
Do you think I can hold in my hand?"

…Now, that is a question that only the Lord can Answer…
"How many flowers can a little girl hold in her Hand?"…
…Enough to fill the heart of her father…
…With one left over
…To rest upon the soul…
And serve as a gentle reminder
Of the abundance
Of God's love…

Passing Thoughts...
To Ponder

&

A Tribute to
Women
and
Romance

Last evening,
I asked my kids to put their shoes on
As we would be leaving…

A few minutes went by
And I realized that I heard silence…
(With young children, silence should always prompt
Parental investigation!)

I looked around the kitchen doorway at the foyer…
And saw my seven year old son
Teaching my four year old daughter
How to tie her shoelaces…

I just stood there…silently…
For a few minutes…
And watched…
And listened…
And smiled…
…with a tear in my eye…

…I am truly blessed…

Passing Thoughts...
To Ponder

&

A Tribute to
Women
and
Romance

Lord...grant that my heart
May have the strength
To endure the mightiest of storms...
And the gentleness
To care for the precious feelings
Of a child

The confidence of a child
Is worth far more
Than any fortune the world has to offer...
Protect it...
Treasure it...
In doing so...the child will learn trust
...a gift which knows no end...

Passing Thoughts...
To Ponder

&

A Tribute to
Women
and
Romance

The sound of the ocean may stir the heart…
Yet, one quiet teardrop on the face of a child
Touches the soul at its depths

Children are our greatest 'natural resource'…
Let us cherish them

Let us plant the seeds of love
On the fertile soil of a child's heart…
Let us sprinkle it with the waters of kindness…
Shine the light of the Lord upon it…
And surround it with the air of compassion…

Let us then watch it flourish…
And revel in its beauty

Passing Thoughts...
To Ponder

&

A Tribute to
Women
and
Romance

A Tribute to
Women and Romance

Passing Thoughts...
To Ponder

&

A Tribute to
Women
and
Romance

A Tribute to Women

If one examines most writings pertaining to the 'greatness' of women, what is found is a litany of accomplishments by famous women throughout history.

This book is not intended to serve as a litany; for by its very essence, such prose, while inspirational, implies that true greatness is rare.

I beg to differ.

This book is not about great accomplishments of women; it's about the greatness of women.

It has amazed me that so many women fail to see their own true beauty.

By 'beauty', I'm not referring to pulchritude; I'm referring to that specific quality representing a culmination of a multitude of attributes.

Alone, these attributes are considerable.

Together, they assume a character that is nothing short of extraordinary.

It's a travesty that society has succeeded in making women feel as though they aren't 'beautiful' unless they look like a covergirl.

I have known many beautiful women in my life, and not one among them was able to see herself as anything more than 'average'; and that is a shame.

So, it naturally begs the question:

Why do so many women fail to see their own beauty?

Passing Thoughts...
To Ponder

&

A Tribute to

Women

and

Romance

Physical Details

Go to any grocery store in the country and stand in the check-out line.
You're surrounded by a myriad of women's magazines that almost
invariably have a photograph of a woman on the cover.
By that very photograph, a statement is made:
"This is the current definition of 'beautiful', and any aberration from this
is less so."
Many women, particularly young women, look at that photograph
and instantly start a comparison between the image on the cover and
themselves.
To what, exactly, are they comparing themselves?
A set of impossible physical standards.
But whose standards are they?
Many manufacturers of cosmetics, clothing, shampoos, and the like
would have women believe that these are society's standards:
and if they would simply purchase those products,
or follow the advice in the articles contained therein,
they, too, could be 'beautiful'.
In reality, however, women are already beautiful, they just don't see it.
To clarify, I'm not saying that these women on the covers aren't pretty,
for they are.
But, they can't compare to the beautiful women whom I've known.

Passing Thoughts…
To Ponder

&

A Tribute to
Women
and
Romance

The Reflection

What happens when many women look in a mirror?

They generally look to the one or two areas that are of most concern to them.

Areas that they attempt to cover with make-up, reduce or augment,

diminish or accentuate.

I told a woman, once, that I wished she could, even for a brief moment,

have the ability to see in herself what I saw in her.

There would be times that she would tell me that she could see something

special in my eyes when I would look at her…

And I would reply that what she was seeing

was her own reflection.

Mirrors have no soul and no heart.

They are pitifully incapable of reflecting the true beauty

that exists within a women,

and should not be relied upon for anything but the most

basic of requirements.

The true beauty that a woman portrays,

is not the image that is reflected in a mirror.

It is the beauty that exists within her heart.

Passing Thoughts…
To Ponder

&

A Tribute to

Women

and

Romance

Denial of Beauty

In working with children and young adults on a daily basis,
I've realized that many young women have a difficult time stating
their strengths.
It's as though they are fearful of sounding egotistical.
So much so, that they, oftentimes, belittle their talents.
They do this so frequently, that it almost becomes second nature.

They have an equally difficult time accepting compliments.
Many times, in my office, if I pay a compliment to a child, the mom
will look at her child and ask, "What do you say?";
expecting to hear the reply, "Thank you."
This is encouraging, as it indicates the acknowledgement of personal
strengths.
If we could continue to encourage this in our young people today,
perhaps the women of tomorrow will be better able to see their own
true beauty.

Passing Thoughts…
To Ponder

&

A Tribute to

Women

and

Romance

Hallmarks of True Beauty

We've spoken of 'true beauty'…
So, what is it that makes a woman truly beautiful?
As was stated earlier, true beauty is a specific quality
representing a culmination of a multitude of attributes.

I assure you that mere words will not adequately describe these attributes,
for they are more easily perceived than described.
But I shall do my best.

Femininity and Strength

Somewhere along the line (and I'm not exactly sure when or
how this occurred), the concept arose that a woman's 'femininity'
and her 'strength'
were mutually exclusive attributes.
It was feared that if she behaved as a 'lady', that she would be
'pushed around' in the corporate setting.
It was also feared that if she portrayed her 'strength', that she would
be viewed as less than 'lady-like'.
These are absolute and preposterous myths.

Passing Thoughts...
To Ponder

&

A Tribute to

Women

and

Romance

In fact, one of the most attractive attributes that a woman possesses is her ability to demonstrate femininity and strength at the same time.

I've known a number of women who hold positions as physicians, medical directors, corporate vice-presidents, and the like.
Each and every one of those women are very well-respected by their supervisors, peers, and subordinates alike.
They are 'ladies' in every sense of the word, and they are able to display incredible strength, without at all diminishing their femininity.
In fact, I believe that a woman's strength adds to her femininity.

If you don't believe me, look to nature for proof.
The next time you see a rose, examine it carefully.
The first thing you notice are the petals,
vibrant and delicate.
But upon what do those petals rest?
A stem, with strength to withstand the winds of life;
leaves, to assure its nourishment, that it may survive;
and thorns, for protection against ill will…
None of these characteristics diminishing the beauty of the petals…
In fact, in its entirety, they add to the overall true beauty of the rose.
But the beauty doesn't stop there.
For it is only when one approaches the rose,
that they are able to smell its sweet fragrance…
The unique fragrance that sets the rose apart from all the flowers of the earth.

Passing Thoughts...
To Ponder

&

A Tribute to
Women
and
Romance

The Smile

It is in a woman's smile that one can see
Her true spirit, her heart, and her soul.

I've known women whose smile could turn my entire day around.
A smile that, although I had seen it a hundred times before, would still
Cause my breath to catch for an instant.

I assure you that these women could have run circles around any 'covergirl'
in the world, as far as I'm concerned.
These women smiled with their eyes.
Their entire face would illuminate,
and suddenly, everything around them
would briefly disappear from view.
But it's not only how a woman smiles that is so enchanting,
it's when she smiles.
You can see a woman who appears to be having a very busy day,
with one child in her arms, and a second child holding onto her hand,
two feet behind her, giggling in the rain, and trying to step in every puddle
in the parking lot on the way to the car.
And yet, you look up at the woman's face…
and she's smiling…
at a time, possibly, when she realizes that it's either smile or cry.
There…is a truly beautiful woman.

Passing Thoughts…
To Ponder

&

A Tribute to
Women
and
Romance

Charm

Now, if I were able to adequately define the constituents of a
woman's charm,
then I would be the best author on earth.
And since there's no chance of that,
this definition, again, will be far from adequate.
But I shall put forth my best effort.

A woman's charm isn't actually a characteristic; but rather,
it's an aura which surrounds her.
Within that aura, lies her intelligence, her wit, her sense of humor,
her kindness, her gentleness, her ability to endure hardship,
her love, and her hope.

If one is attentive,
This aura can be appreciated the moment a woman enters a room.
It can be seen and felt...in her actions and in her words,
both spoken and written.

It is this aura, the mere presence of her, that can turn something as simple
as a spartan dinner served on a 'table' of cardboard boxes on moving day
into the most romantic of meals.

Passing Thoughts…
To Ponder

&

A Tribute to

Women

and

Romance

Romance: The Truth and the Myth

Ok…I admit that I'm a 'hopeless romantic', the dangers of which are well-known.

But, if that's not bad enough, I'm also an eternal optimist.

Not the best combination if you're interested in keeping your heart in one piece

at all times; but I've always been willing to risk a few scars on my heart for a chance at romantic fulfillment.

There exists a myth that 'true romance' is found only in the movies.

The fact remains… 'True romance' can exist in 'real life', as well.

You just have to take advantage of individual 'moments'.

There is no such thing as a perfect relationship.

That being the case,

there aren't going to be many (or any) perfect weeks or days in a relationship.

But, there can exist perfect 'moments'.

You just have to be able to recognize them when they appear, and take advantage of them before they slip by.

I'll share with you a couple of examples…

Passing Thoughts...
To Ponder

&

A Tribute to
Women
and
Romance

Several years ago, a young woman and I were enjoying a day together
in a beautiful little village in autumn.
The air was slightly brisk, the skies were blue, and the leaves were at their peak
in fall colors of red and gold.
There were sidewalk musicians playing romantic music;
and as we passed, I tuned to her, took her into my arms,
and started dancing with her.
Couples, young and old, gathered around and watched us dance.
When the song ended, we thanked the musicians, and continued on our way.
I wouldn't trade those two minutes of my life for all the money in the world.

Passing Thoughts…
To Ponder

&

A Tribute to
Women
and
Romance

One evening, after a particularly difficult day at work, I stopped by
to see the woman I was dating at the time.
She could tell that I had had a long day.
It was early summer, at dusk, and she suggested we eat dinner
out on her front porch.

I took some steaks out to the grill, while she prepared the salad and
side dishes.
I brought a small table out to the porch. She lit a candle
and turned on some music, while I poured the wine.
And as the sun dipped completely from view,
and the stars overtook the evening sky, we enjoyed a beautiful dinner.

After we finished eating, I took her hand
and we danced in the warm night air…
Saying so much to each other with silent glances into each other's eyes.
To this day, I can smell her perfume;
I can see that candlelight flickering against the white pillars of her porch…
Again, a perfect 'moment' in time…

The keys to those 'perfect moments' are as follows:

Passing Thoughts…
To Ponder

&

A Tribute to

Women

and

Romance

1.   Recognize those opportunities when they present themselves.

There's a rule in medicine… "You can't find what you don't look for."
You have to look for those opportunities, and occasionally, you have
to create your own, because they don't always magically appear.

2.   Don't wait to take advantage of those opportunities.

If you wait too long, the opportunity will pass. Recall my first example:
If that woman and I had continued to walk down that street,
while I was deciding whether or not to dance with her;
within two minutes, the song would have ended,
we would have already passed the musicians…
and it would have been too late.
And she and I would be shy one memory at the end of our lives.

Passing Thoughts...
To Ponder

&

A Tribute to

Women

and

Romance

3.   *Enjoy the spontaneity.*

We spend so much of our lives 'planning'. It's absolutely necessary
in many situations, and there's a lot to be said for it.
But have you ever noticed that some of the most enjoyable times of your life
were not planned?

When I lived in France, I went to Nice for a week on vacation.
While there, I passed by the train station.
There was a train about to leave for Monaco.
I hadn't planned that as part of my trip, but I wanted to go.
So, I bought a ticket, and a half-hour later, I was in Monaco.

Monaco has to be one of the most beautiful places on the face of the earth.
But half the pleasure was in the spontaneity.

It's the same way with romance.
You enjoy the moment,
and you enjoy the spontaneity that leads to the moment.

Passing Thoughts…
To Ponder

&

A Tribute to

Women

and

Romance

4.   Don't worry about being the center of attention for a moment.

Recall my first example again: Those couples standing around
(mostly older couples) had the biggest smiles on their faces,
and many of them clapped afterwards.
Perhaps, many of them wanted to do the same thing.

I believe that there are a lot of couples who thirst for romance,
but when an opportunity like that arises,
they 'chicken out' at the last minute.
Don't chicken out!

5.   Be an 'Ice-breaker'.

A couple of years ago, a band was playing in the midst
of a huge shopping mall.
There was a small dance floor around the stage, but no one was dancing.
I asked the woman whom I was with to dance.
At first, she was a little reluctant, but she had a great spirit.
She decided to be 'brave', and go out onto that dance floor with me.
Within 3 minutes, there were about a dozen couples out there with us.
Sometimes, people just need someone to break the ice.
Don't be afraid to be an 'ice-breaker' when it comes to romance.

Passing Thoughts…
To Ponder

&

A Tribute to
Women
and
Romance

6. Be willing to put forth a little time and effort…It's important!

I met a woman about a year ago.
There was something about her, the first time I saw her.
She had one of the most charming faces I had ever seen in my life.
When she smiled, there was this progression of radiance
which moved from her lips…to her cheeks…to her eyes…
all within a second or two.
Shortly after we met, I discovered that I had just missed her birthday.
So, I printed out a scripted formal invitation:

"The honour of your presence
is cordially requested at a dinner
being held in your honour,
in belated celebration of the
anniversary of your birth"

I prepared a five course dinner,
complete with wine, candlelight, and music.
(I think she was a little surprised.)
The point is…It took a little time and effort,
but I enjoyed doing it.
Romance is important, and it's easy to lose sight of its importance
In the midst of 'day to day' life.
Don't lose sight.

Passing Thoughts...
To Ponder

&

A Tribute to
Women
and
Romance

7. Put a unique twist on an old theme.

I once wanted to surprise a very special woman
with a dozen long-stemmed roses.
Now, I realized that I could have just put them in a vase…
and that would have been nice…
But instead, I had the girl in the flower shop wrap each one
individually.
I, then, staggered the roses up the walkway leading to the front door,
awaiting her return home from work.
When she walked in, the final rose was in a vase.
It just takes a little thought…

Passing Thoughts...
To Ponder

&

A Tribute to

Women

and

Romance

8.   Don't forget the 'little things'…for they are not little!

Not everything 'romantic' has to involve extravagance,
or significant time and effort.
I'm speaking of those 'little things'.

The reason they mean so much is because they reflect a thought
in the midst of an otherwise 'typical busy day'.

I've done things as simple as leaving a card on her windshield,
so it would be there when she left work; or writing 'I love you'
with shaving cream on the bathroom counter.

It doesn't take much effort,
but I like to think of the smile on her face…
something, hopefully, that will break up her day,
and let her know that I'm with her in spirit.

Passing Thoughts…
To Ponder

&

A Tribute to
Women
and
Romance

So, why did I write this tribute?

A couple of reasons, actually...

Firstly, I've known many truly beautiful women in my life...
one of whom, I married.
The marriage didn't work out,
but that hasn't changed the fact that she's beautiful,
and I couldn't have found a more wonderful mother
for our two children.

It's just rather disheartening when a beautiful woman
doesn't realize that she's beautiful.

I wanted to put into words
what I see in a woman,
in the hope that any woman reading this
will start seeing those things in herself.

Secondly, sometimes I fear for the future of romance...
It's becoming a lost art.
We've begun to lose our focus.
Life has gotten so busy, that the concepts of romance and chivalry
almost have been forgotten.

Passing Thoughts…
To Ponder

&

A Tribute to
Women
and
Romance

Hopefully, this book will prompt a revitalization,
a 'new age' of 'old-fashioned' romance.

And let's not forget chivalry…
The concept of holding doors open for a woman,
and giving up your seat if a woman is standing…
I know that some women may look at these actions as demeaning,
but I've always viewed them as a sign of respect.

As I wrote earlier in this book:
"Simply because society has finally accepted the obvious fact
That women are equally competent as men;
That does not imply that they should be treated
As anything less than a woman…
Let us celebrate the inherent differences…
Let us remember that chivalry
Is a sign of respect…"

Passing Thoughts...
To Ponder

&

A Tribute to
Women
and
Romance

I was fortunate to grow up in a house with seven siblings,
six of whom were sisters.
My father taught me, at a young age, to hold the door
for my sisters and mother.
And I'm grateful for that.

My father was the epitome of class…
A man of quiet dignity,
who possessed the strength to show compassion,
the greatness to show humility,
and the wisdom to teach by example.
I had a great role model.
I only hope that I can do half that well.

Printed in the United States
34672LVS00011B/151-153